MY HERO

Sally's Snow Adventure

Written and Illustrated by

Stephen Huneck

Abrams Books for Young Readers
New York

Thank you to all the talented people at
Harry N. Abrams, David Glentz Brush, and most
of all Sally for continuing to inspire me!

Production Manager: Alexis Mentor

Library of Congress Cataloging-in-Publication Data:
Huneck, Stephen.
Sally's snow adventure / by Stephen Huneck.
p. cm.
Summary: Sally, a black Labrador retriever, becomes lost in the
woods while on a winter vacation.
ISBN 10: 0-8109-7061-9
ISBN 13: 978-0-8109-7061-8
[1. Labrador retriever—Fiction. 2. Dogs—Fiction. 3. Rescue
dogs—Fiction.] I. Title.

PZ7.H8995Sc 2006
[E]—dc22
02005021160

Printed and bound in Singapore
10 9 8 7 6 5 4 3 2 1

HNA ▮▮▮▮
harry n. abrams, inc.
a subsidiary of La Martinière Groupe
115 West 18th Street
New York, NY 10011
www.hnabooks.com

VERMONT SNOW ANGELS

To brave rescue dogs everywhere,
thank you for doing your job so well

We are driving to a dog-friendly lodge.
It looks like everyone is going. I stick
my head out the window and catch
snowflakes on my tongue.

As soon as we pull in we are greeted by two guests. They say the lodge is almost full. Come in and meet the rest!

Since I have just arrived,
everybody wants to greet me.

With so many different dogs,
there is a lot of sniffing going on.

We check into our room. It is
very late. The bed is just like mine
at home. I fall right to sleep.

A wonderful smell wakes me up.
Something is baking in the kitchen.
I think I will go and investigate.

In the dining room, I am happy to hear:
"Breakfast is served!"

We are all on our best behavior.

Outside, I meet two dogs wearing handsome vests. "My new friends and I are going sledding. Would you like to come?"

"Sorry, Sally. We are rescue dogs and we are working now. We find lost skiers. Remember to stay on the trail, so you will not get lost."

My new friends and I race to
get on a sled. We are having so much
fun that we go again and again.

We try saucering next. It is
quite a thrill. You spin around and
around and go fast down the hill.

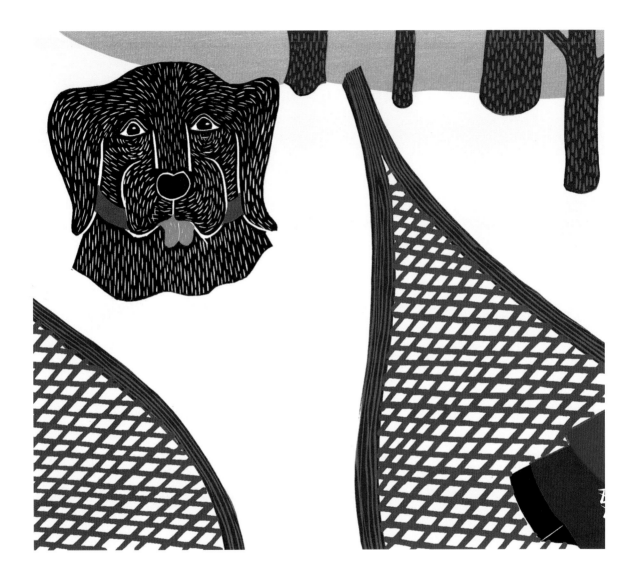

Snowshoeing is good exercise.
It makes me very thirsty.

I am glad Emma brought some
water to share with everyone.

I love snowboarding. The wind is
whistling in my ears. I feel like
I am flying!

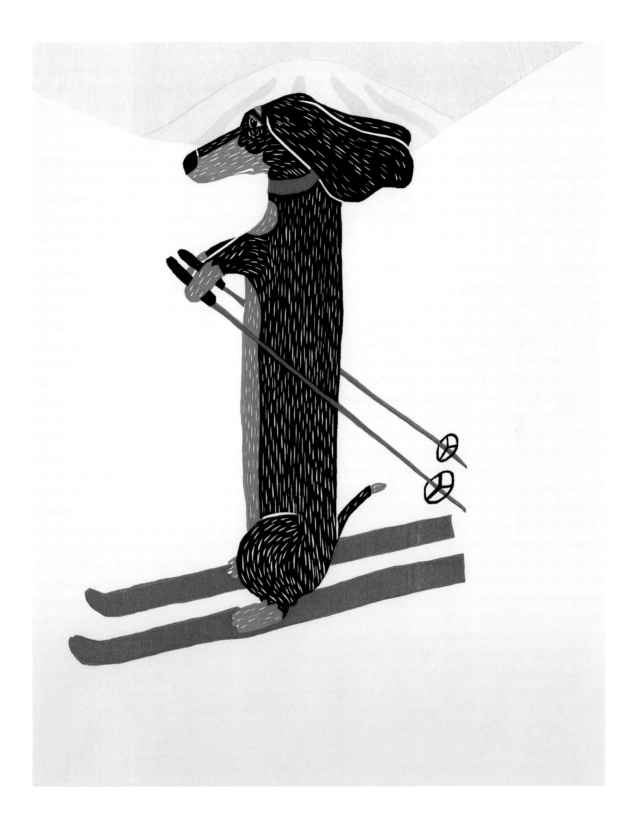

Skiing looks like fun. I think I will try that next. Look at that hot dog go!

I see skiers being pulled by
a rope, so I grab ahold too.

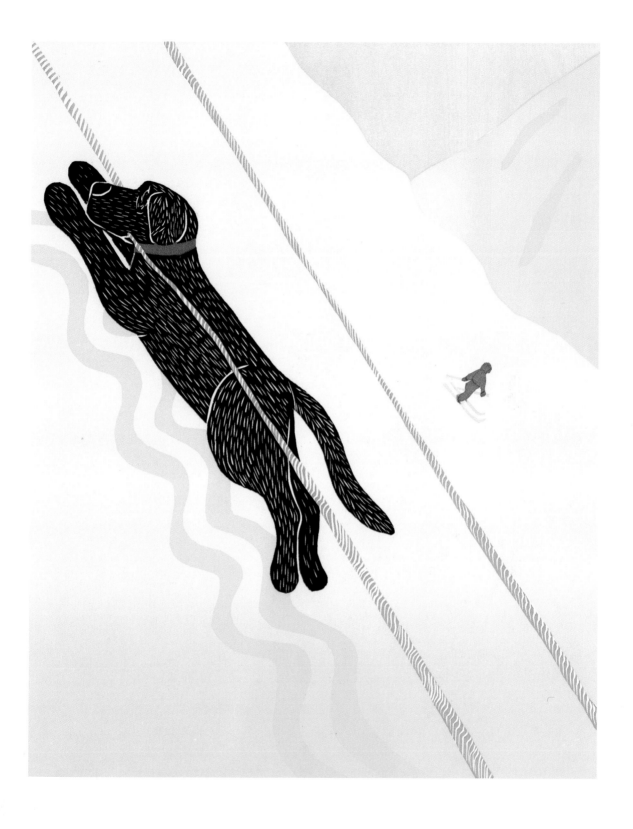

But I have no skis so I go
bump, bump, bump all the way up!

I am enjoying the beautiful sunset
when my stomach starts to growl.

It must be almost dinnertime. I should get back to the lodge. I will take a short-cut through the woods.

I wish I had listened to the rescue dogs and stayed on the trails. I have been walking and walking and am tired. And lost!

Sally's new friends ask one another, "Where is Sally?" "It is not like Sally to miss a meal." "We better tell the rescue dogs. Sally might be lost!"

The rescue dogs say, "Let's go! Let's go!"

"We know just what to do."

"We will follow Sally's tracks in the snow."

"MY HEROES! MY HEROES!
You found me!" Sally exclaims.
"How did you know I was lost?"

"Why, your new friends told us," the
rescue dogs explain. To keep me warm,
they snuggle up close all the way
back to the lodge.

"I am so glad to be back. Thank you to all my new friends for looking out for me."

"And a special thank-you to the rescue dogs for doing their job so well."

"Come on everybody, something smells good. We still have time for dinner."

MY HERO